Indonesian Children's Favorite Stories

FABLES, MYTHS AND FAIRY TALES

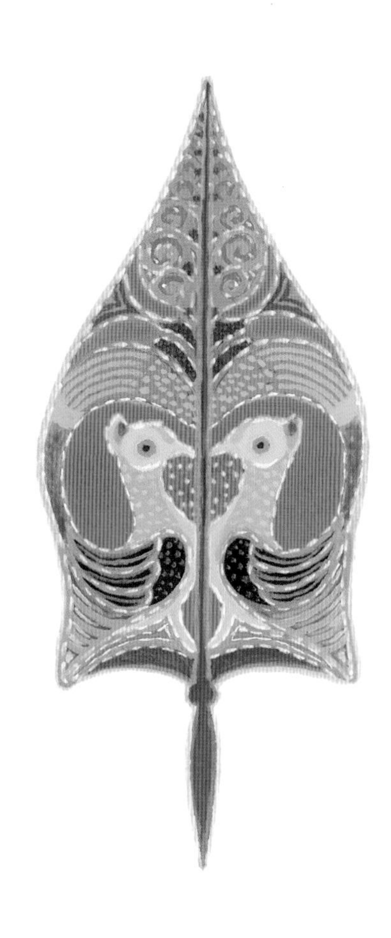

Indonesian Children's Favorite Stories

FABLES, MYTHS AND FAIRY TALES

Text by Joan Suyenaga
Illustrations by Salim Martowiredjo

TUTTLE Publishing
Tokyo | Rutland, Vermont | Singapore

The children of Indonesia occupy a vast archipelago stretching from the northern tip of Sumatra to the border of west Papua. Representing more than 300 ethnic groups, they share an incredibly rich heritage of stories and dreams. Although Kancil, the mousedeer, is indigenous only to parts of Sumatra and the neighboring Malay Peninsula, stories about this clever trickster are known by children throughout the archipelago and are amongst the most famous stories in the islands. Also popular are stories where an agile mind outwits brute strength and greed, where the truth of the spoken word becomes reality, and where dreams come true because one's heart is true. Children live the lives of the princesses, princes, woodcarvers, and wandering teachers of these stories. They save their villages, rule as wise kings, outsmart giants and ferocious beasts, and win their true love, in their imagination. Through these fantasies they learn that real magic lies in the values of honesty, determination, cleverness, patience, and bravery.

—Joan Suyenaga

To my mother, who taught me "the world is yours."
—Joan Suyenaga

For all children, the inheritors of the world.
—Salim Martowiredjo

Published by Tuttle Publishing, an imprint of
Periplus Editions (HK) Ltd.

www.tuttlepublishing.com

Library of Congress in Process
ISBN 978-0-8048-5150-3

24 23 22 21 20 19
10 9 8 7 6 5 4 3 2 1 1908EP

Printed in Hong Kong

Distributed by:
North America, Latin America & Europe
Tuttle Publishing
364 Innovation Drive, North Clarendon,
VT 05759-9436 U.S.A.
Tel: 1 (802) 773-8930: Fax: 1 (802) 773-6993
info@tuttlepublishing.com
www.tuttlepublishing.com

Asia Pacific
Berkeley Books Pte Ltd
3 Kallang Sector #04-01
Singapore 349278
Tel: (65) 6741 2178: Fax: (65) 6741 2179
inquiries@periplus.com.sg
www.periplus.com

Indonesia
PT Java Books Indonesia
Kawasan Industri Pulogadung
JI. Rawa Gelam IV No. 9, Jakarta 13930
Tel: (62) 21 4682-1088; Fax: (62) 21 461-0206
crm@periplus.co.id
www.periplus.com

Contents

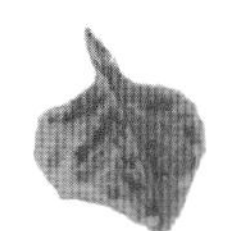

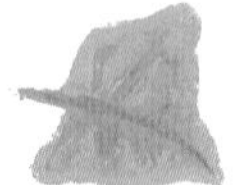

True Strength

Long ago there lived a wise, humble and clever man named Patih Senggilur. He was famous throughout the land not only for his skills and honesty, but for his supernatural strength as well. Many villagers would seek his advice in settling arguments.

Patih Senggilur spent all of his days and nights amongst the villagers so that he could understand their lives. He never wasted time, but rather spent it wisely making and fixing things or tending to his rice fields. He was a role model for all of the villagers who listened to his advice. No one dared to contradict or challenge him. Since he spent so much time in the village, he knew everyone and everything that happened.

At this time, there were three men who roamed the country. They were strong, arrogant and supernaturally

powerful. Sharp weapons could not penetrate their skin. Unfortunately, these men misused this power for selfish purposes. They would attack whoever they met on the road and rob them of their goods, jewelry and weapons. The thieves would challenge their victims to try to strike them with their knives or swords. If they could not be hurt, then the thieves would take their victims' weapons. With their supernatural power, they could not be struck, so the thieves took all the weapons. They became known as the "weapon traders."

The villagers became afraid of traveling. If they had to go out, then they would not take any weapons with them, although that was risky as there were other dangers, such as wild animals, on the road.

One day, when Patih Senggilur and several other villagers were weaving mats out of strips of rattan by the side of the road, three men approached. With loud, rough voices, they challenged the villagers.

"We are the weapon traders! Who amongst you dares to fight us?"

Patih Senggilur remained calm. The villagers were silent too.

Angrily, the rogues repeated their challenge. "Hey! Who amongst you dares to fight us?"

The silence that greeted them made them even more furious. They had traveled far that morning and were very tired. Sweat poured down their faces.

Patih Senggilur calmly invited the men to sit down.

"Come, sit down. The sun is hot and you are exhausted. You have journeyed far today and you must be tired. I have some cucumbers and watermelons that will refresh you. When you have eaten your fill and you are refreshed, you may tell us why you have come here."

There was no reply, and Patih Senggilur quietly returned to his work weaving the rattan mat while glancing cautiously from time to time at the rogues.

Hot, thirsty and hungry, the thieves were tempted by the cucumbers and watermelons offered to them. Hesitantly, they looked at each other. Patih Senggilur laughed to himself, then again offered the cucumbers and watermelons to them.

"Why do you hesitate? Come, eat! The cucumbers and watermelons will quench your thirst and satisfy your hunger. If you finish these, I will fetch more for you. I have many more inside. The cucumbers are from my own fields. Come, eat! Don't be shy!"

Hearing this second offer, the thieves quickly rushed to grab the cucumbers and watermelons. They fought loudly with each other to see who could get the most and piled them up in front of themselves.

They took out their knives and daggers to slice the cucumbers, but were dismayed to find that their sharp knives and daggers could not cut through the cucumber skin. No matter how

hard they tried, the cucumber skin would not peel off, nor could it be cut. They were so busy trying to cut the cucumbers that they were not aware that Patih Senggilur was casting glances at them.

He laughed silently, keeping his thoughts to himself, "Ha, ha, ha! Now you can see how it feels to be weak. I hope this is a good lesson for you. It seems that the power you show off to everyone else means nothing to me. You can't even peel one ripe cucumber!"

Patih Senggilur pretended not to see the thieves as they struggled. They tried to chop and cut, and chop and cut, but the cucumbers remained whole. The sweat poured down their faces and bodies as they tried all of their weapons. Next they tried to cut up the watermelons but to no avail.

Finally, Patih Senggilur looked up.

"But why haven't you eaten? I don't have anything else to offer you. Please go ahead, eat them. Don't be shy."

The three thieves did not answer. They just looked at each other and then at Patih Senggilur. Patih Senggilur looked back at them.

"Alright, if you insist, I'll cut them up for you." He then took the small knife he used to shave the bamboo and rattan strips for making mats. He wiped it against the palm of his left hand three times, then began to cut up the cucumbers and watermelons. The knife moved easily and swiftly, like a hot knife through butter. In just a few seconds, the cucumbers and watermelons were cut into equal slices, placed on a plate, and presented to the amazed thieves.

"There, I have cut them up for you. Go ahead, eat them."

The three thieves could do nothing except stare at each other and at the cucumbers and watermelons. They realized that they were in the presence of someone with great supernatural power, power far greater than theirs. They bowed their heads and without saying a word, turned and left the village. They learned humility in the presence of true strength.

The Woodcarver's True Love

King Simbau, the king of the island of Simbau in the Sulawesi Sea, had a beautiful daughter. Her name was Sangiang Mapaele. The princess was not only beautiful, but she was also wise and kind.

Three princes from neighboring islands had proposed marriage to her. Many rich merchants also wished to marry the princess.

Her father, the king, was confused. Who should be his daughter's husband? The king wanted to choose the best husband for his daughter. But how would he do this? He decided he would choose whoever loved the princess the most.

King Simbau then announced a contest. Whoever—nobleman or commoner—presented Princess Sangiang Mapaele with the most valuable gift as a sign of his love, would marry the princess. The announcement of the contest was spread far and wide throughout the island and the neighboring islands as well. Commoners did not dare to enter the contest. Who amongst them had anything of value for the king's daughter? But Takatuliang, a poor woodsman, decided to try. For many years he had harbored a love for the princess deep in his heart. Now was his chance to express the love that had remained hidden for so long.

Takatuliang thought very long and hard. Finally, he went far into the forest. There, he chose a tree of the finest grain and cut it down. For days he labored without tiring, not even going home at night.

After several days, his elderly mother went in search of him in the forest. When she found him hunched over this work, she wiped the sweat from her son's brow and asked, "Takatuliang, Takatuliang, what are you doing in this forest that is so important that you forgot to come home?"

Takatuliang answered, "I am working, Mother, for the king's daughter."

The next day, his mother returned to the forest and again asked, "Takatuliang, Takatuliang, what are you doing that is more important than returning home?"

Takatuliang answered, "I am working, Mother, to prove my love."

His mother was shocked to hear this. Now she knew that he intended to propose marriage to the princess. Her heart ached.

"Takatuliang, oh Takatuliang, child of my heart! Come to your senses, my son. All you have is the skin on your bones!"

Takatuliang said, "That is why I am working. I am creating proof of my true love."

The next day, his mother returned again. She watched her son as he bent over the piece of wood, shaping it carefully. His face was calm and focused on his work. Pearls of sweat formed on his forehead. Again, she spoke to him gently. "Takatuliang, you are breaking my heart. You are not in your right mind. Stop dreaming. You cannot win the princess. Your rank is so low, and hers is so high. Surely, you will be scorned."

Takatuliang answered again, "Oh, Mother, suffering is only for those who do not exert any effort, for those who deny their God-given gifts. I have energy. I have talent. I have dreams.

And I have a love that can even change the fate of a man."

His mother was silent. She realized that Takatuliang was determined. The only thing she could do was to pray to God to protect her son. Takatuliang smiled as he watched his mother. He rose to wipe the tears from her cheeks, then he guided her out of the dense forest.

The young man continued to shape the piece of wood into a simple doll. He carved the eye sockets, the nose, the delicate lips. He carved intricate designs to represent fine clothes. He searched the forest for two small dry seeds for the eyes and colored the lips with a dye made from the bright red kesumba plant. Only when the doll was finished did Takatuliang go home. At home, Takatuliang pondered over the doll. It was far from perfect. He wondered whether the princess would accept a wooden doll with no hair or clothes. Surely she would laugh at this simple doll and its maker.

Takatuliang then took an old piece of woven cloth, the only thing he had which had belonged to his dead father, and he sewed it into a dress for the doll.

Then he cut his own beautiful wavy hair. Using wood resin, he glued it strand by strand to the doll's head. Now the doll was absolutely perfect.

On the day of the contest, all of the princess's suitors gathered before the king and the beautiful princess.

The three princes, resplendent in their fancy jackets, sat in front. The wealthy merchants, displaying their riches, sat behind them. Only Takatuliang, in his simple rags, sat far at the back holding his wooden doll.

The first and most handsome suitor, the prince of the island of Tatelu, approached the throne. He said proudly, "Dear princess, this is the proof of my love—a comb carved of ivory and inset with sparkling opals."

Princess Sangiang Mapaele examined the comb and asked, "How many combs like this do you own?"

"Oh, very many, my princess. I have ten chests full of them."

Then, the princess turned to the second suitor and asked, "And you, sir, what is your proof of your love?"

The prince of Darua island spoke proudly, "This cloth of exquisite pure silk is proof of my love."

Princess Sangiang Mapaele asked him, "How many pieces of silk like this do you have?"

The prince answered, "Oh, very many. Closets and closets full!"

It was then the third prince's turn. He, the prince of Epa island, presented her with a stunning necklace of gold and diamonds.

Princess Sangiang Mapaele asked him, "And how many necklaces like this do you have?"

The prince answered, "Oh, very many. I have five boxes jam packed with them."

Following the presentations of these fine gifts by the three princes, the rich merchants then had their chance to show their offerings to the princess. Finally, it was Takatuliang's turn. He crept forward reluctantly.

Princess Sangiang Mapaele saw him and asked, "What have you brought as proof of your love for me?"

Bowing his head low, Takatuliang spoke softly, "I bring only a doll."

"How many dolls like this do you have?" asked the princess.

Takatuliang whispered, "Only this one. I carved it from a tree in the forest. I decorated it with my own hair. I wrapped it in my father's cloth. If I had more hair and cloth, then I would surely make more dolls for you, princess."

"You mean that this doll's hair is yours? And the clothes are from your father's cloth?" asked the princess.

"Yes, princess," answered Takatuliang. "My father died and this is the only piece of cloth, indeed the only thing in the world that he left for me."

Princess Sangiang Mapaele was very touched to hear this, as was her father.

Turning to his daughter, quietly the king asked, "My dear, have you made your choice? Who will be your husband?"

"Only Takatuliang has proven his love. I choose him," answered the princess.

All of the princes and merchants were shocked. "My lord, this is not fair!" they shouted. "Why has Princess Sangiang Mapaele chosen him? Why has she refused our expensive gifts and accepted a simple ugly wooden doll?"

King Simbau was a wise man and he calmly spoke to the enraged suitors. "I agree with my daughter's choice. Your presents have no real value. All of you have many of the items you presented, and yet you chose to bring only one. Look at Takatuliang. He brought only one doll wrapped in a worn piece of cloth, but it has much greater value because he has given everything he has—his own effort, his father's simple inheritance, and even his own hair—a true gift from the heart. He has made a sacrifice for love."

The princes and merchants were silent. They felt very ashamed. The fabulously expensive jewelry, the magnificient cloth, the goods that they were so proud of had no meaning compared with Takatuliang's simple wooden doll. They gathered up their belongings and left.

Takatuliang stayed and married Princess Sangiang Mapaele in a grand ceremony.

Together their love for each other grew and grew with each passing day.

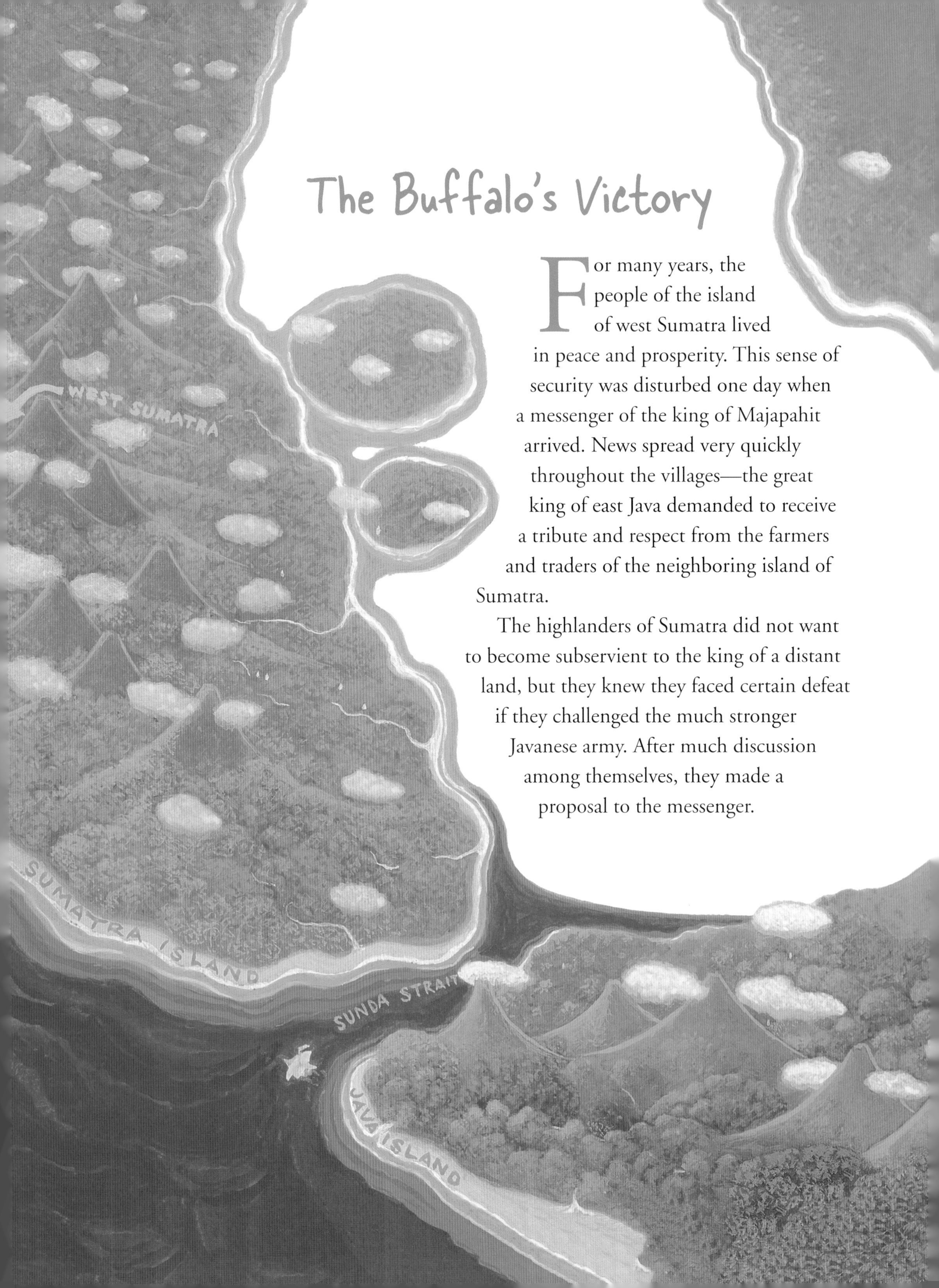

The Buffalo's Victory

For many years, the people of the island of west Sumatra lived in peace and prosperity. This sense of security was disturbed one day when a messenger of the king of Majapahit arrived. News spread very quickly throughout the villages—the great king of east Java demanded to receive a tribute and respect from the farmers and traders of the neighboring island of Sumatra.

The highlanders of Sumatra did not want to become subservient to the king of a distant land, but they knew they faced certain defeat if they challenged the much stronger Javanese army. After much discussion among themselves, they made a proposal to the messenger.

Rather than a battle of armies and the loss of many lives on both sides, the west Sumatrans proposed that their fate be determined in a battle between buffaloes representing each side. If the Sumatran buffalo lost, then they would recognize the authority of the king of Majapahit and pay tribute to him. However, if the Sumatran buffalo won, the Javanese army would leave the highlands immediately and never force their presence in the land again.

This proposal was taken back to the king of Java. After lengthy discussion with his advisers, the king agreed to the proposal. A search was then carried out to find the biggest, strongest and most powerful buffalo on the island of Java. When they had chosen their champion, the Javanese army began their journey through the jungles, over the mountain passes, across the Sunda Strait, and through the dense rainforest of Sumatra.

The Sumatran villagers were awed and dismayed at the sight of the mighty Javanese buffalo. Again, they gathered to discuss their options and strategies.

Surely, they would lose if the battle between the buffaloes was one of pure strength. Instead, they decided they had no choice but to place their fate in the power of nature. One of the villagers had a buffalo who had recently given birth. They took the newborn calf and separated it from its mother for several days.

The village square was roped off for the all-important battle. People from distant villages in the highlands also came to watch, anxious to witness the fight that would determine their fate—independence or servitude.

The powerful Javanese buffalo stood majestically at one end of the field, as if reveling in his own magnificence. A group of villagers arrived leading the young calf, weak with hunger. Sharp iron tips shaped into the horns of a full-grown adult buffalo were strapped onto the tiny humps where the calf's horns would later grow.

The Javanese army could not believe their eyes. Their own mighty champion facing this small feeble baby! They roared with laughter while the Sumatrans waited quietly, keeping their hopes and despair to themselves.

A hush fell over the rowdy crowd as they witnessed the meeting between the two mismatched buffaloes. At first, the young calf just stood still, bewildered, at the far end of the field. Then he spotted the other buffalo. His heart leapt. Perhaps it was his mother, for whom he longed.

Three days without milk—and finally, there was his mother! He rushed straight on ahead toward the massive buffalo. When he reached him, he tilted his head under the champion's belly in search of milk. The sharp iron horns pierced the buffalo's belly.

With a squeal of pain, the champion bolted away, but the calf followed him, desperately seeking milk and piercing the belly over and over again. After receiving countless wounds, the mighty Javanese buffalo finally collapsed on the ground, blood pouring out of its wounds. This time it was the Sumatran villagers who roared with a cry of victory, "Minang! Minang! Victory! Victory!"

The Javanese soldiers, dazed and speechless, collected the carcass of their buffalo and left the highlands, never to return.

To this day, the victory of the buffalo, or kabau, is celebrated in the name of the highlanders of west Sumatra, the Minangkabau. The roofs of their homes and the shape of their formal headcloths take the form of buffalo horns to commemorate their victory over the mighty Javanese.

The Magic Headcloth

Many, many years ago, the kingdom of Medangkamulan was ruled by a much feared and ferocious king named Dewata-chengkar. This king had a strange and frightening habit—he liked to eat human beings! Every month he had to have at least one human being to eat. He especially liked those who were young and chubby. The problem for the king's advisers was how to provide their ruler with enough humans to satisfy his craving.

At first, the advisers took people from the countries they had conquered, but eventually they had to look for victims from among their own people. Every month, the soldiers would travel through the villages to select and capture the next victims. The people of Medangkamulan were terrified of the king and his army.

One day, a young traveler arrived in the kingdom. The stranger stood tall and straight. He was kind and clever

and was well-received by the villagers. At first, they thought that he would serve well as the next victim, but they took a liking to the young man. He was called Ajisaka.

Ajisaka took shelter in the house of a widow who quickly came to look upon the young man as her own son. Ajisaka began to teach the villagers. He also listened to the villagers' problems and often helped them find solutions.

When he heard of the king's strange appetite, Ajisaka sympathized with their plight and immediately volunteered to become the king's next meal.

Ajisaka went directly to the king's palace. He boldly announced to the king that he was willing to sacrifice himself.

"I am willing to be your next meal, Your Highness. However, I have a request."

Dewata-chengkar was pleased. Ajisaka was young and strong. He would make a tender and filling meal.

"Whatever you please, young man, I will grant your request," the king replied.

"Before you eat me, grant me some land. Just enough for my own grave."

"Ha ha ha! Your own grave? I will give you enough land for many graves!"

"Oh no, Your Majesty. I just need land that is the length of my own headcloth."

The ferocious king laughed again and agreed to what he thought was a very strange request.

"This you shall have. Come, let us measure your headcloth so that I can have my meal and you can have your grave!"

With this, Ajisaka began to unwrap the cloth tied around his head. The king got down from his throne and took hold of one end. He stepped backward, thinking that the cloth would unravel to the usual length of one meter. What he didn't know was that this headcloth was much longer than usual!

The king kept going backward, step by step, as the cloth kept unraveling. He stepped backward through the palace square, backward across the village marketplace, backward down the length of the village and backward through the countryside. People gathered, amazed at the sight of their king walking backward through the kingdom, holding the end of Ajisaka's headcloth.

Dewata-chengkar was mystified. He was a king and he had to keep his promise. A king's word is final. He could do nothing other than measure the length of the headcloth and grant the land to Ajisaka. He kept stepping backward the length of his kingdom until finally he reached the sea cliffs of the Southern Seas.

By now, a great crowd had gathered. They held their breath as their king took his final step backward over the cliff's edge and plunged into the waves crashing against the rocks at the foot of the sea wall. A victorious roar rose up as they watched their greedy king disappear under the waves.

The crowd returned to the palace with Ajisaka and thanked him for his courage, cunning, and magical powers. They made him their new king. To this day, Ajisaka is remembered as the wise ruler who later brought the knowledge of letters to the Javanese.

Kancil Steals Cucumbers

One day, while wandering through the rainforest, Kancil, the mousedeer, came to a clearing in which there was a field filled with ripening cucumbers. Kancil was thrilled as he loved to eat cucumbers and these were large and juicy, not like the wild ones he occasionally found in the forest.

He ate until he was full, then fell asleep in the bushes at the forest's edge. The next day was another day of feasting for the clever mousedeer.

On the third day, the farmer and his wife came to tend to their vegetables, only to find that many of the cucumbers had been eaten. Kancil hid behind a bush and watched the furious farmer throw up his hands in desperation.

"Arrgh! These cucumbers were ripe and ready to be picked! Now there are only bits and pieces scattered all over the place! It must have been a wild pig or some forest creature that ate our cucumbers," the farmer shouted while waving his arms in the air. "Watch out, you thief!" he cried to the unseen animal. "The day I catch you will be your last!"

Kancil was amazed. He had never seen humans before and he was impressed with the way the farmer jumped up and down, shouting and waving his arms in the air. Finally, after harvesting a few cucumbers, the farmer and his wife left the field. They planned to return in a few days to harvest the rest.

Kancil celebrated again. He would take a few bites out of one cucumber and then leave it to bite into another fresh, juicy one. When he had his fill, he retired under the bushes at the edge of the field.

When the farmer returned two days later to check the field, he found most of the cucumbers torn from the vines and bitten. The field was in ruins.

"Ah, this thief is definitely not a human. It must be an animal. I will set a trap," he thought.

The next day, the farmer returned carrying a large doll which he had covered with a sticky resin from the jackfruit tree. He placed it on a stick in the middle of the cucumbers and left the field.

Upon seeing this new figure, Kancil thought, "Ah hah! More people. The farmer has brought a friend. But this one looks so stiff. He's really not as lively as the farmer."

Kancil wondered why the friend was left in the field and not taken home with the farmer. He watched the doll and saw how it moved only when the wind blew. He decided that this human, unlike the farmer, was a dull, ignorant fellow. Kancil approached it. As the figure did nothing but wave in the wind, Kancil became braver and began to run around it. "How stupid I am! This human can't even walk, much less run. Why should I be afraid?"

Kancil took a closer look. He stared right into its wide, unmoving eyes. "Huh! He doesn't even blink. Why this isn't even a human at all! It's a doll put here to scare me. Why should I be scared of something that can't move? I'm not even scared of tigers or crocodiles, so why should I be frightened of this doll?"

Emboldened by the revelation, Kancil approached the doll. He taunted it. "Here, I'll give you some cucumbers. If you move, I'll kick you!"

Playfully, Kancil kicked the doll which was covered with sticky resin. His paw stuck to the doll's body! "Hey, hey! You brute! How dare you hold on to my paw! Let me go or I'll hit you!"

Kancil struck the doll with his front paw and … it stuck as well. "Hey, this is crazy! Now you're holding on to my other paw! Come on, let me go! Let me go! If you don't, I'll hit you again!"

Kancil, now desperate, began to kick with his remaining free paws, but only succeeded in getting all four paws stuck to the doll. He could do nothing except stare up at the clouds in the sky or down at the remaining cucumbers in the field. He was completely stuck and had to stay there for the rest of the day. Late in the afternoon, the farmer returned to the field. Seeing that he had succeeded in trapping the cucumber thief, he rejoiced. "Ah hah! I've caught you! You'll be very delicious when we've cooked you up in a stew!"

The farmer plucked Kancil off the sticky doll, put him in a bamboo cage and took him home. Deciding to have Kancil cooked in the morning, he left the cage in the yard for the night. He put a heavy stone on top of the woven bamboo cage so that it could not be easily overturned. Kancil was so distraught he could do nothing but lie quietly.

In the middle of the night, when the farmer and his family had gone to sleep, Kancil lay awake thinking. He spotted the family's watchdog lying near the cage. Kancil called out softly to the dog, "Sst! Dog, come here! Let's be friends. I'm the new family pet. Did you know that the farmer's son is so fond of me that he's going to take me to town tomorrow to see the big festival that the chief is sponsoring."

Skeptical, the dog answered, "Hah! I don't believe that. I've been with them for many years and they've never taken me to town."

"Believe me or not, it's up to you. You can believe me or you don't have to believe me.

But if you really are interested, I can arrange it so that you can go too." Kancil said nonchalantly.

Now the dog perked up. He did want to go to town. "Yes, I'd really like that!"

"That's easy. All you have to do is join me in this cage. When the farmer's son comes, I'll ask him to take you too. I'm sure it will be okay. See if you can get this stone off the top of the cage and join me," Kancil said.

The dog did as he was told. He knocked the stone off, tipped the cage back and slid under to join Kancil inside. At the same moment, in one quick movement, Kancil slipped out of the cage and ran back to the forest. He called out, "Dog, I hope that you are invited to go to the town tomorrow morning and not made into stew! Just wait there patiently!"

The dog, confused, didn't understand what had just happened. By the time he realized that he had been tricked, Kancil was already safe, deep in the heart of the forest.

The Frog and the Magic Axe

Nestled in the southeast corner of the Banda Sea are the tiny islands of the Kei archipelago. The Kei islanders live by fishing and sea trading.

On one of these islands long ago lived a widow and her seven sons. Six of the sons were healthy and handsome boys, but her youngest child was born in the shape of a frog. They called him Katak, the frog.

Katak was a brave, hardworking and thoughtful son. Although his mother loved him dearly, his brothers often made fun of him and did not allow him to join in their fun and games.

There came a day when the six brothers decided that they would go on a long fishing trip. They also wanted to venture to other islands to trade.

When he heard of their plans, Katak asked if he could join them. At first, the older brothers objected, but Katak persisted and at last they agreed to let him go along.

When they were loading the boat with food and fishing supplies, Katak asked only for a ripe watermelon and his mother's blessings.

The journey began smoothly as the winds were full, but gentle.

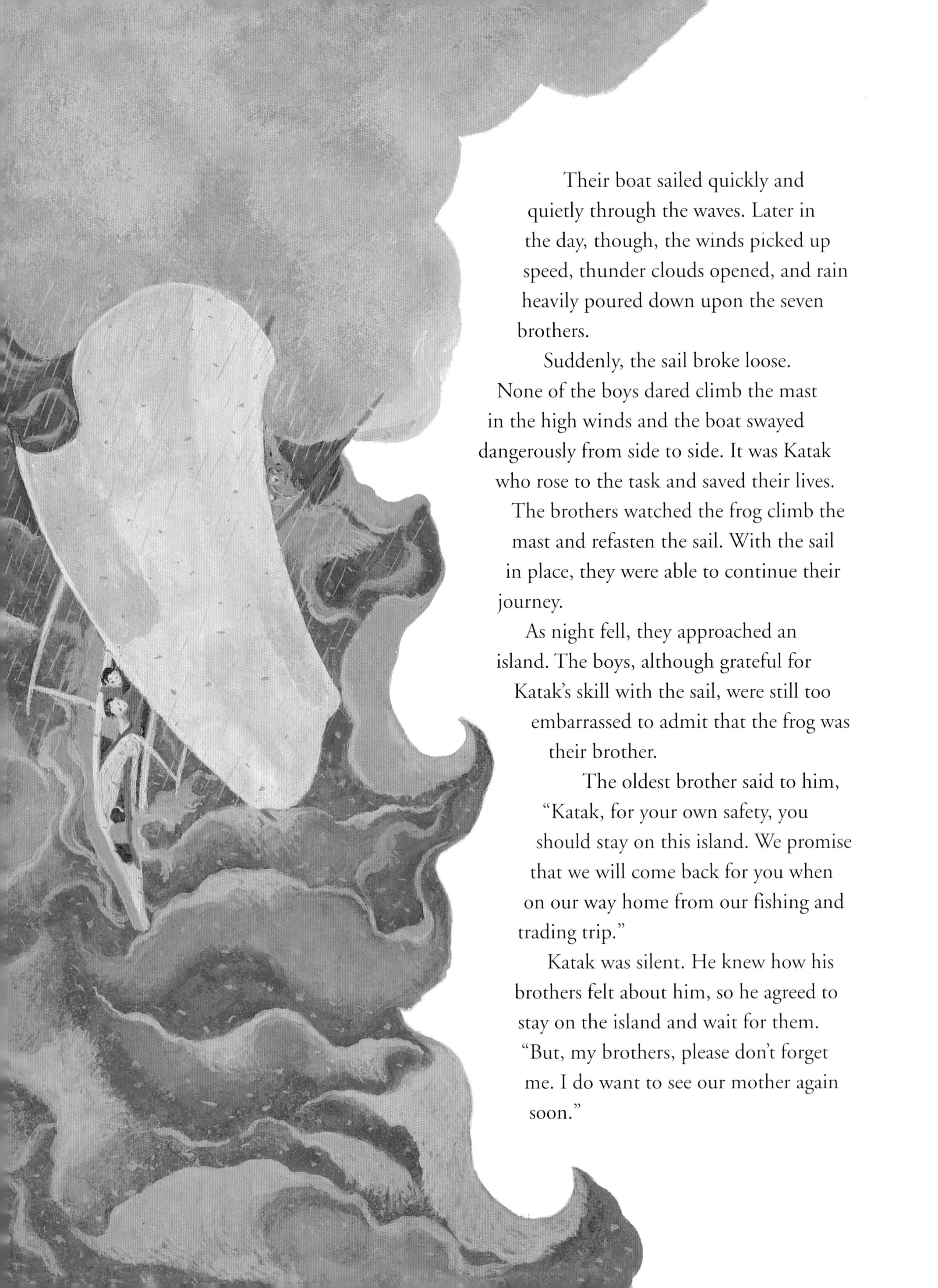

Their boat sailed quickly and quietly through the waves. Later in the day, though, the winds picked up speed, thunder clouds opened, and rain heavily poured down upon the seven brothers.

Suddenly, the sail broke loose. None of the boys dared climb the mast in the high winds and the boat swayed dangerously from side to side. It was Katak who rose to the task and saved their lives. The brothers watched the frog climb the mast and refasten the sail. With the sail in place, they were able to continue their journey.

As night fell, they approached an island. The boys, although grateful for Katak's skill with the sail, were still too embarrassed to admit that the frog was their brother.

The oldest brother said to him, "Katak, for your own safety, you should stay on this island. We promise that we will come back for you when on our way home from our fishing and trading trip."

Katak was silent. He knew how his brothers felt about him, so he agreed to stay on the island and wait for them. "But, my brothers, please don't forget me. I do want to see our mother again soon."

In the morning, as soon as it was light, the brothers left the island and Katak began to build a house and garden for the duration of his stay. He also planted the seeds from the watermelon his mother had given him. The soil was fertile and the vine grew quickly. Soon Katak had many watermelons ripening in his garden. But as soon as the melons ripened, however, they disappeared from the vine. Katak was very puzzled. He had never seen anyone else on the island, and yet someone was taking his fruit. He decided to lay a trap for the thief.

That night, Katak waited quietly under a leaf. Soon a large and frightening tree spirit emerged from the darkness. His eyes glowed red and his mouth curled up into a bone-chilling smile as he spotted a ripe watermelon.

Just as the spirit's long, gnarled fingers reached out to pick the fruit, Katak jumped onto the spirit's back and wrestled with him. Although the tree spirit was much bigger than the frog, Katak was quick and clever, so that in a just a few seconds he had tied the tree spirit up with loose vines.

"So, YOU are the thief!"

"Ow! Aaahhh! Oww! Owwww!" screamed the tree spirit. "I'm sorry, I'm sorry! I did not mean to steal! I see only the melons. I see not their owner.

I know only the melons. I know not their owner. They are so juicy, so sweet!"

Tree spirits, though terrifying to look at, are not known for their courage. Katak, as small as he was, had the daring and strength of a hundred tree spirits.

"Oww! Let me go! Let me go! If you let me go, I will pay you for all the melons. I will pay you very handsomely."

"Hmmm ... what can you pay me with, spirit?" Katak asked.

"Ahhh, I have a magic axe. You have but to strike it three times and it will fulfill any wish you make. This I will give to you for the melons."

Katak was pleased with this. He untied the vines and released the tree spirit.

"Here, you are free to go. Give me the magic axe and the watermelon garden is yours."

A few days later, Katak was walking on the beach where he had landed several months previously. Suddenly, he spotted a black dot on the horizon. As it got closer, he saw that it was his brothers' boat. He jumped up and down and waved frantically. But to his great disappointment, the boat did not turn toward the island to pick him up as his brothers had promised.

Katak decided that this was a good time to test his magic axe. He struck the axe against a coconut tree three times and made a wish. All of a sudden, the wind stopped blowing. The boat came to a standstill and could go no further. The brothers had no choice but to turn around and head for the island. As soon as they decided this, the wind picked up again and the boat quickly approached the beach where Katak waited. He boarded the boat and they all sailed home.

Katak's mother was delighted to welcome her seven sons home. She was shocked, though, when Katak approached her a week later and asked her to go to the king's palace and propose a marriage with one of the king's daughters.

"What? My son, how is it possible that the king's daughter will consent to marry a frog? How can you even dare to hope for this?"

"Fear not, dear Mother. Just do as I ask."

The devoted mother did as her youngest son asked her and visited the palace the next day. She asked the king if one of his daughters would marry her son who was a frog. Needless to say, the king dismissed her immediately.

Katak was not discouraged and asked his mother to repeat the request a few days later. She tried to convince her son that it was hopeless, but he would not listen to her. So she went again to the palace and again was dismissed.

At Katak's insistence, she went one more time to plea for acceptance.

This time the king's youngest daughter, Bungsu, spoke."I will marry your son, the frog, if he prepares a carpet of the finest woven mat that leads an unbroken path from your house to the palace. Along both sides of the path must stand the strongest of warriors armed with spears and shields. Finally, he must present me with baskets overflowing with gold, diamonds and pearls. If your son can give me all of these things, then I will marry him."

Katak's mother returned home distraught. How could her poor son ever hope to offer such a bride price? The king and his daughter surely did not expect them to fulfill this demand. They were mocking him.

However, Katak was delighted with his mother's report. He told her not to worry and to prepare for the wedding.

The next morning, Katak's mother and brothers were amazed to wake up and see everything the princess had asked for—the mat, the warriors, and the jewels. The king and everyone in the palace were equally astonished.

Bungsu, true to her word, married Katak that very day. She came to enjoy his presence as he was kind and thoughtful. He could make her laugh and dry her tears.

But Katak never accompanied his wife when she attended formal receptions and family gatherings, as he knew she was too embarrassed by his appearance.

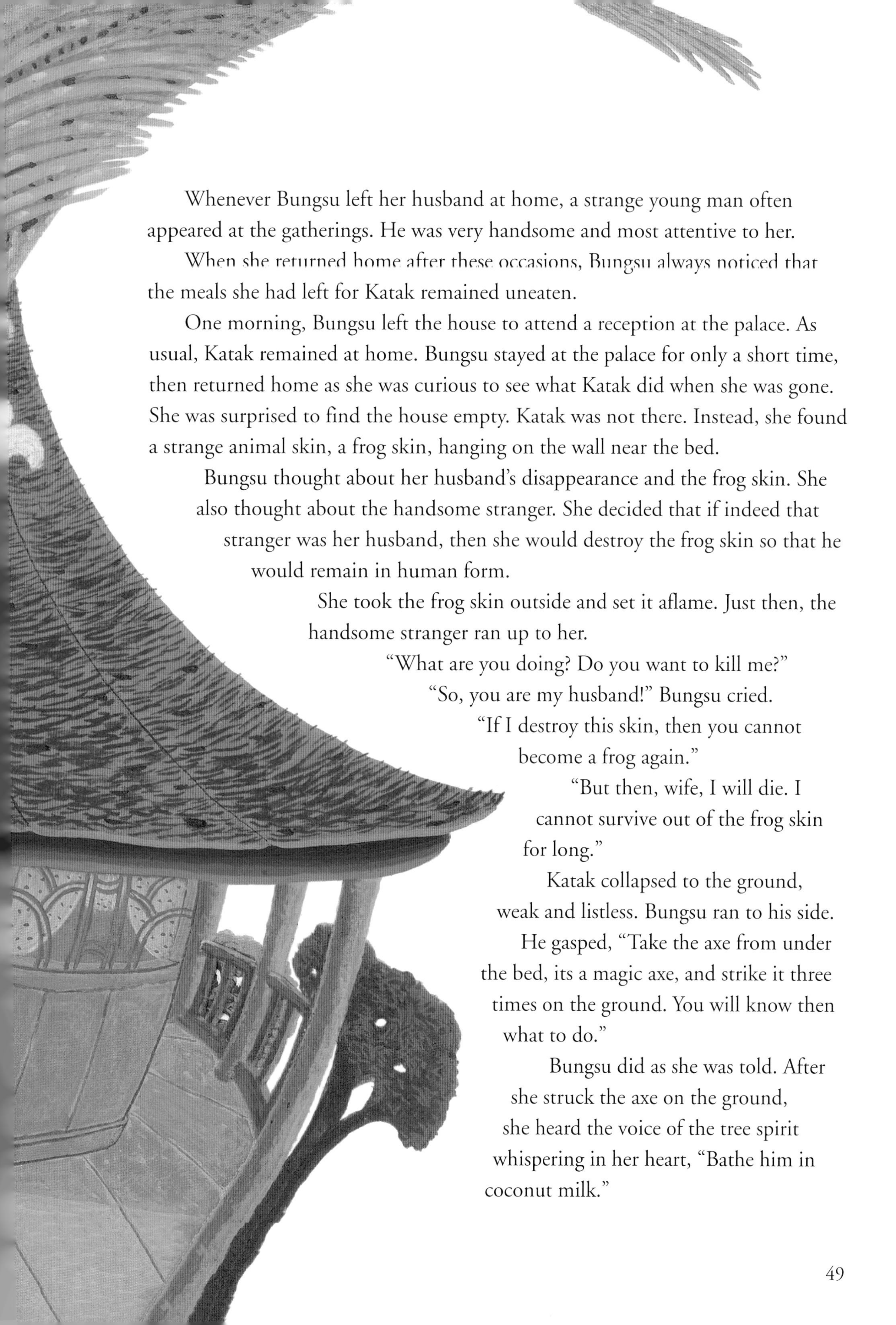

Whenever Bungsu left her husband at home, a strange young man often appeared at the gatherings. He was very handsome and most attentive to her.

When she returned home after these occasions, Bungsu always noticed that the meals she had left for Katak remained uneaten.

One morning, Bungsu left the house to attend a reception at the palace. As usual, Katak remained at home. Bungsu stayed at the palace for only a short time, then returned home as she was curious to see what Katak did when she was gone. She was surprised to find the house empty. Katak was not there. Instead, she found a strange animal skin, a frog skin, hanging on the wall near the bed.

Bungsu thought about her husband's disappearance and the frog skin. She also thought about the handsome stranger. She decided that if indeed that stranger was her husband, then she would destroy the frog skin so that he would remain in human form.

She took the frog skin outside and set it aflame. Just then, the handsome stranger ran up to her.

"What are you doing? Do you want to kill me?"

"So, you are my husband!" Bungsu cried. "If I destroy this skin, then you cannot become a frog again."

"But then, wife, I will die. I cannot survive out of the frog skin for long."

Katak collapsed to the ground, weak and listless. Bungsu ran to his side. He gasped, "Take the axe from under the bed, its a magic axe, and strike it three times on the ground. You will know then what to do."

Bungsu did as she was told. After she struck the axe on the ground, she heard the voice of the tree spirit whispering in her heart, "Bathe him in coconut milk."

Quickly, Bungsu gathered as many coconuts as she could find. She cracked them open using the magic axe, carved the white flesh from the shell, grated it, and squeezed the flakes to get thick, white coconut milk. She poured the milk into a wooden bowl, took it to her husband and bathed him in it.

Gradually, his short, uneven breaths grew deeper and more even. His body warmed and his strength returned. Slowly, he opened his eyes and he gazed upon his wife, his heart bursting with love.

"Thank you, my sweet wife. You have saved my life. You loved me when I was a frog, but those days are now over. Can you love me as a human?" he asked.

"My dear husband, I grew to love you for your kind heart and quick mind, your willingness to work hard and your tenderness in caring for me. If you are still all of this, then I will love you forever," Bungsu answered.

Katak smiled tenderly. "Come, my precious Bungsu. We can now walk proudly in the sunlight together." And this they did with much happiness and love.

The Caterpillar Story

Once upon a time there was a wise and beloved chief. He lived a simple life in his longhouse. He would open his compound to his people who would gather in the grounds to talk and enjoy themselves under his protection.

One young boy often played in the compound, as the simple hut in which he lived with his widowed mother sat right on the river bank and offered no place for a child to play. While gathering roots in the rainforest one day, he found a caterpillar of bright colors. He gently picked up the caterpillar with a broad leaf and carefully carried it home.

The next day, after he had finished some chores for his mother, he took the caterpillar to the chief's compound to show to his friends.

There he played until the sun disappeared behind the trees and it grew dark. In his rush to run home, the boy left the caterpillar on one of the steps of the chief's longhouse. The chief decided to take care of the little creature until the next day.

When the young boy returned to the chief's longhouse the next day, he was horrified when he was told that his pet caterpillar had been eaten by the chief's rooster. The poor boy who had so little had lost his one prized possession. His tears flowed silently.

Taking pity on the poor boy, the chief gently said to him, "Here, take this rooster to replace your caterpillar."

Delighted with this unexpected offer, the boy clutched the rooster in his arms and ran home to show his new pet to his mother.

He returned later that afternoon with the rooster to play with his friends. The rooster was let loose to roam freely. As he did every day, the rooster approached the chief's servants who were pounding the rice grains in preparation for the evening meal. He pecked at the grains that fell on the mat at the side of the lesung, the long wooden mortar where three servants pounded the rice rhythmically with long wood sticks. The bold rooster even tried to peck at the rice inside the lesung, but he was shooed away by the servants. This deterred him only momentarily and when the pounders took rest again, the rooster approached the lesung again. This time, one of the servants struck out at the bird with the rice pounding stick and hit its head soundly. The rooster fell limp and died.

Sadly, the boy picked up his rooster and took it to the chief. The chief gazed down at the boy and said, "Take the rice pounder in replacement for your rooster."

"Sir, thank you for your most generous gift. My mother's hut is small and there is no place to store this rice pounder at the moment. May I leave it here in your care overnight so that I may clear a corner of the hut for it?" the boy asked timidly.

"Of course, my son. Stand it up next to that jackfruit tree," answered the chief while pointing to a tall tree heavy with enormous spiky fruit.

The next day, when the boy returned to claim the pounder and take it home, he found it lying on the ground, shattered into a thousand pieces. Next to it lay an enormous overripe jackfruit which had fallen from the tree and split open.

When the boy went yet again to the chief, the latter smiled patiently.

"Alright, my boy, take this jackfruit in place of your pounder. It should provide you and your mother with food for several days."

"Thank you," the boy answered, "I will, but it is already getting dark. If I take it now, I cannot run home and my mother will worry. Please may I leave it here in your care and I will return for it tomorrow morning."

"Yes, place the jackfruit over by the kitchen door."

The boy dragged the heavy fruit to the back door and left it there from where its pungent aroma spread through the longhouse.

Later that night, the chief's daughter began to crave jackfruit.

"Ahhhh, the aroma tempts me! If it were still on the tree, then I would climb it right now to pick a ripe one. I want to eat some right now!"

The chief's daughter then took a knife and immediately cut up the jackfruit placed on the kitchen doorstep. She devoured much of the jackfruit raw and then ordered her servant to cook the rest for the morning's meal.

The next day, when the boy looked up to the chief in request for payment for his jackfruit, the chief sighed and shook his head. "When your caterpillar was eaten by my rooster, I gave you the rooster. When the rooster was killed by the rice pounder, I gave you the rice pounder. When the rice pounder was smashed by the jackfruit, I gave you the jackfruit. And now, when my daughter has eaten your jackfruit, there is nothing that I can do other than give you my daughter. When the two of you are old enough, she will be yours to marry."

And so it was, that when the young boy grew to manhood, he married the chief's daughter and, in time, became the chief of the village, and like his beloved wife's father, governed in wisdom and kindness.

The Story of Timun Mas

Many, many long years ago, there lived a farmer and his wife. They worked diligently in their fields and prospered. They were content with their lives but for one thing—they longed for a child to cheer up their quiet home. For many years they prayed to God to grant them a baby girl or boy, but sadly no child was born to bless their lives.

Eventually, the farmer's wife, determined and desperate, decided to venture forth to beg for help from the demon spirit of a distant forest. She journeyed far and deep into the heart of the forest until she arrived at the demon's cave.

When the demon emerged from the cave, she almost ran away, so scared was she by the sight of him, but her longing for a child was greater than her fear of the spectacle she faced. The terrifying giant was as tall as a towering coconut tree, had huge round eyes, a bulging nose, and sharp fangs which glistened at the sides of his gaping mouth. Shaggy, tangled hair covered his immense body and the ground shuddered with his every step. A terrible odor came from his body.

"You have disturbed my sleep, woman!" the giant roared. "I know why you have come. You are lonely. You dare to ask my help? You dare to ask for a child?"

The farmer's wife was so petrified that she could not speak. She could barely breathe. The demon threw his head back and roared with laughter.

"Ha, ha, ha, ha! You may have your child, but on one condition. If it is a boy, then you may keep him. I have no use for boys. But if the child is a girl, then you must return her to me when she is fifteen

years old. Do you understand? Do you agree to this condition?"

The farmer's wife thought quickly. If the child were a boy, then there would be no problem. But if it were a girl, then she and her husband still had fifteen years to find a way to outwit the demon. She nodded slowly in agreement to his condition.

"Ha, ha, ha, ha! Then take these cucumber seeds. Tend them well." The woman gingerly took the seeds from his huge, pawlike hand, then turned and scurried home as fast as she could, relieved to be away from the hideous sight and stench of the demon.

As soon as she reached home, the farmer's wife planted the cucumber seeds in a garden near her cottage. She watered and tended them with care, and it was not long before a healthly vine sprang up. Soon there were many luscious cucumbers growing on the vine, but she and her husband were quick to notice that there was one which was much bigger than all the others. It was golden in color and it seemed to radiate a glow at night.

When this special cucumber was ripe and ready to pick, the farmer and his wife very carefully broke it open. Inside the cucumber was a beautiful baby girl. They named her Timun Mas, which means Golden Cucumber. They were delighted with their new child and loved her dearly.

Fearing the day when the demon would appear to reclaim their child, the farmer and his wife asked the advice of an old hermit who lived on a high and distant mountain. The kind hermit gave them a pouch filled with a needle, some salt and a chunk of fish paste with instructions that

Timun Mas should throw these behind her one by one if she were ever pursued by the demon.

At dawn on the day of Timun Mas's fifteenth birthday, the farmer and his wife told their beloved daughter about the demon and his demand and gave her the pouch from the hermit. Timun Mas hugged her parents, then ran off into the northern forest.

Later that morning, the demon appeared at the cottage of the farmer and his wife.

"I have come for the child. Where is she? I want her now!" he roared.

"Ah yes, Timun Mas," the farmer replied calmly. "We told her you were coming, but she decided she didn't want to stay. She has run off into the forest."

The demon's eyes bulged and his nostrils flared widely.

"She … she ran off that way," said the farmer, pointing to the south, hoping to deceive the demon. The demon turned to the south, but he could sense that the girl was not there. He then turned around and lumbered toward the north in hot pursuit of Timun Mas. His broad strides quickly made up for the distance between him and the young girl.

Exhausted from running, Timun Mas took a brief rest beneath a tree. Suddenly, she noticed small animals scurrying through the bushes and birds fluttering away from the treetops. The ground trembled and she realized that the demon was fast catching up on her. She jumped up and started running again.

As the rumbling grew louder, she reached into the hermit's pouch, picked out the needle and threw it behind her. The instant the needle hit the ground, a forest of bamboo sprouted up. The bamboo stalks grew so densely that the demon could barely squeeze through them and wherever he could, he stepped on razor sharp shoots that pierced his feet. "Oooo, owwww, ouch," he screamed.

The bamboo slowed him down considerably as Timum Mas kept running. Eventually, however, he was able to make his way through the bamboo grove. When Timun Mas heard the demon getting closer, she threw the salt behind her.

Immediately, a vast sea bubbled out of the ground. But this did not halt the demon. He waded, then swam the breadth of the sea, before continuing his pursuit of the girl.

Timun Mas was panting and crying from exhaustion. She reached again into the pouch, picked out the pungent chunk of fish paste and threw it behind her. Instantly, a vast pond of mud bubbled forth.

The demon, without hesitation, plunged into the mud. He had made his way through the bamboo grove, he had swum across the salty sea, surely, he thought, he could wade through the mud pond. He did not know, however, the depth or the suction of the mud, which was much deeper and stronger than he was. Before he had taken three steps, the demon sank down to the bottom of

the mud pond. Quickly and silently, he was swallowed up by the slimy mud.

Timun Mas could hardly believe her eyes. Her tears of exhaustion turned into tears of relief and happiness.

Her parents had followed the demon, but the bamboo forest, salt sea and mud pond had disappeared as the demon passed. When they reached their daughter, they all embraced again, relieved in the warmth of safety.

Timun Mas and her parents walked home together to live in peace and happiness.

ABOUT TUTTLE

"Books to Span the East and West"

Our core mission at Tuttle Publishing is to create books which bring people together one page at a time. Tuttle was founded in 1832 in the small New England town of Rutland, Vermont (USA). Our fundamental values remain as strong today as they were then—to publish best-in-class books informing the English-speaking world about the countries and peoples of Asia. The world has become a smaller place today and Asia's economic, cultural and political influence has expanded, yet the need for meaningful dialogue and information about this diverse region has never been greater. Since 1948, Tuttle has been a leader in publishing books on the cultures, arts, cuisines, languages and literatures of Asia. Our authors and photographers have won numerous awards and Tuttle has published thousands of books on subjects ranging from martial arts to paper crafts. We welcome you to explore the wealth of information available on Asia at **www.tuttlepublishing.com**.

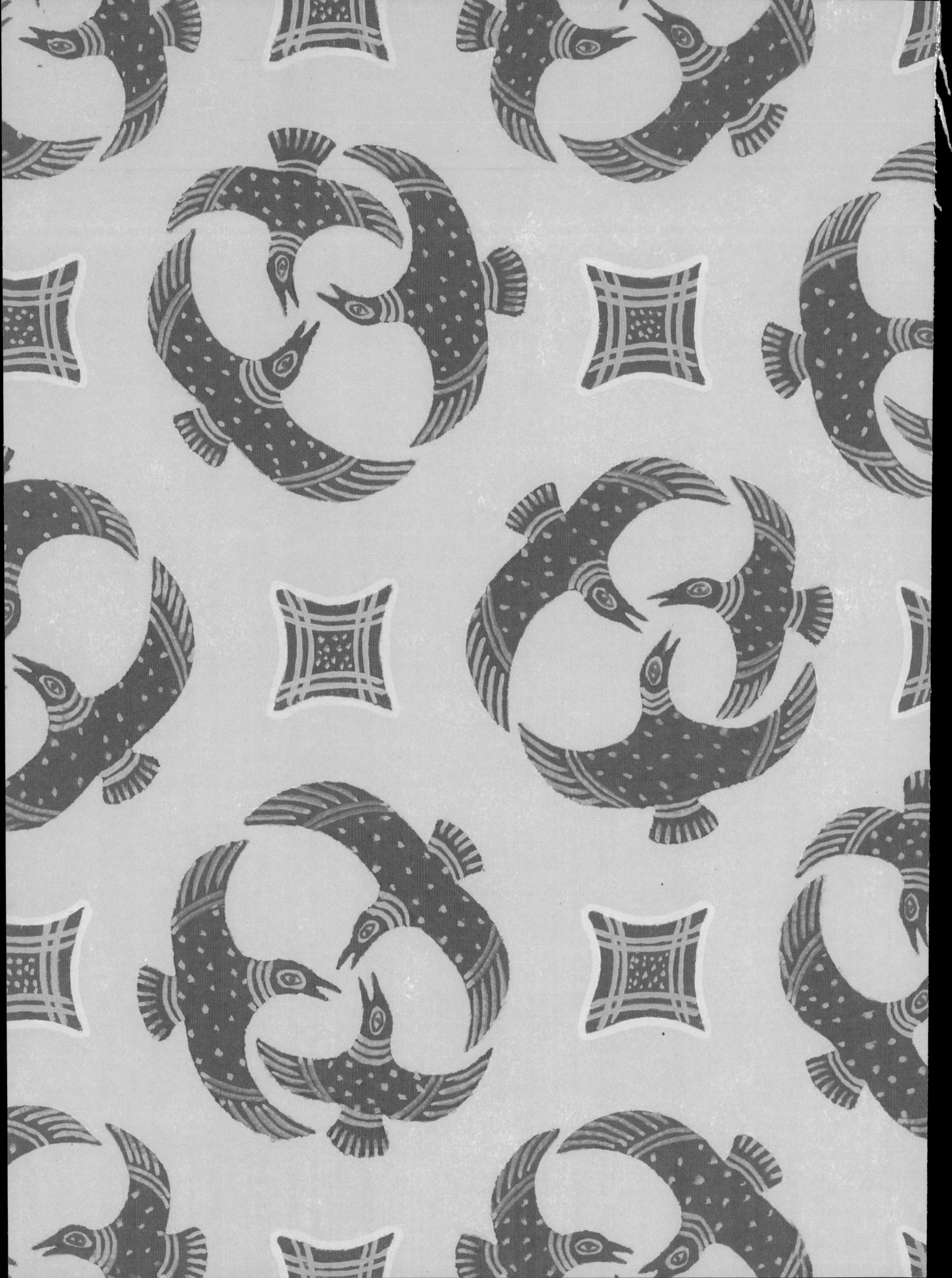